Don't Climb Out of the Window Tonight

by Richard McGilvray

· Illustrated by Alan Snow

Methuen Children's Books

First published in Great Britain 1993
by Methuen Children's Books
an imprint of Reed Consumer Books Limited
Michelin House, 81 Fulham Road, London SW3 6RB
and Auckland, Melbourne, Singapore and Toronto
Text copyright © Richard McGilvray, 1993
Illustrations copyright © Alan Snow, 1993
The moral right of the illustrator has been asserted
Produced by Mandarin, printed in Hong Kong

ISBN 0 416 18629 7

A CIP catalogue record for this book is available at the British Library

Don't climb out of the window tonight because...

crocodiles are in the pond.

Don't climb out of the window tonight because...

goblins are in the grass.

Don't climb out of the window tonight because...

ghosts are flying round your house.

Don't climb out of the window tonight because...

Frankenstein's gang are in the bushes.

Don't climb out of the window tonight because...

witches are behind the wall.

Don't climb out of the window tonight because...

giants are jogging.

Don't climb out of the window tonight because...

Don't climb out of the window tonight because...

dragons are in the drainpipes.

Don't climb out of the window tonight because...

bats are taking their first flying lesson.

Don't climb out of the window tonight because...

Don't climb out of the window tonight...

I would just stay in bed,

wouldn't you?

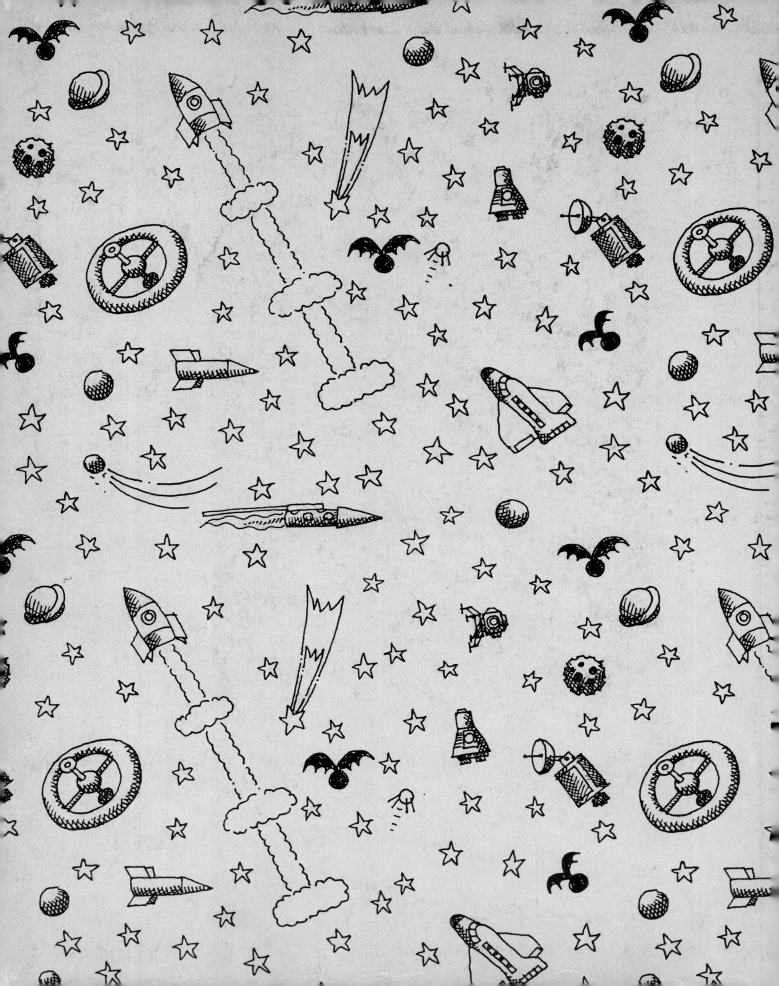